PRAISE FOR ME[illegible]

"[The] undisputed queen of comedy"
—The Toronto Sun

"This caper from Campbell is just that; ridiculous relatives running around and covering up crime after crime. A good read."
—Kirkus Reviews for *The Goddaughter Caper*

"Campbell creates a page-turner that is fast moving, exciting and filled with twists and turns...Highly Recommended."
—CM Magazine for *The Goddaughter Caper*

"Campbell's comic caper is just right for Janet Evanovich fans. Wacky family connections and snappy dialog make it impossible not to laugh."
—Library Journal for *The Goddaughter*

"All that glitters is real gold. Short, sharp and full of what makes a Rapid Read feel like a great cup of coffee."
—The Hamilton Spectator for *The Goddaughter's Revenge*

"A deliciously funny tale"
—VOYA Magazine for *The Goddaughter's Revenge*

"Melodie Campbell is the Queen of the Rapid Read...*Worst Date Ever* is one the best of this genre."
—Canadian Mystery Reviews for *Worst Date Ever*

"This is great for...anyone who enjoys zipping through a lighthearted read."
—Booklist for *Worst Date Ever*

THE B-TEAM

MELODIE CAMPBELL

ORCA BOOK PUBLISHERS

Library and Archives Canada Cataloguing in Publication

Campbell, Melodie, 1955-, author
The B-Team / Melodie Campbell.
(Rapid reads)

Issued in print and electronic formats.
ISBN 978-1-4598-1807-1 (softcover).—ISBN 978-1-4598-1808-8 (pdf).—
ISBN 978-1-4598-1809-5 (epub)

I. Title. II. Series: Rapid reads
PS8605.A54745B74 2018 C813'.6 C2017-904505-9
C2017-904506-7

First published in the United States, 2018
Library of Congress Control Number: 2017949683

Summary: A team of vigilantes seek to right wrongs in this lighthearted work of fiction. (RL 3.1)

Orca Book Publishers is dedicated to preserving the environment and has printed this book on Forest Stewardship Council® certified paper.

Orca Book Publishers gratefully acknowledges the support for its publishing programs provided by the following agencies: the Government of Canada through the Canada Book Fund and the Canada Council for the Arts, and the Province of British Columbia through the BC Arts Council and the Book Publishing Tax Credit.

Design by Gerilee McBride
Cover art by Shutterstock.com/Yorrico

ORCA BOOK PUBLISHERS
www.orcabook.com

Printed and bound in Canada.

21 20 19 18 • 4 3 2 1

For Joan

ONE

We had been summoned. There was no other way to put it.

"Why does she want us?" asked my twin brother, Dino, sitting next to me in the passenger seat of the Mustang.

"No idea." It was baffling. She'd never done this before. And somehow it made me uneasy.

"You nervous?" Dino wriggled in his seat. "I am."

"Ditto." Our great-aunt is a legend in the industrial city of Hamilton, aka The Hammer. You know the expression *cat burglar*? Suffice it to say her nickname in the family is Kitty.

Of course, those infamous burglaries were all long before. Kitty retired a few years ago after breaking an ankle in a bad fall while leaving a second-story window. Now she divides her time between her little house in the forest and the Holy Cannoli Retirement Home, visiting my elderly relatives who reside there. Many of them are dotty. Not Kitty. Her brain cells are in for the long haul.

"Could we have done something wrong?" By wrong, I didn't mean breaking-the-law wrong. Natch. I snuck a glance at Dino.

There was an unfamiliar frown on his otherwise angel-perfect face. "Surely we'd be facing Mom instead."

I shivered.

Nearly there. I pulled into the parking lot behind La Paloma, the upscale bistro owned by our uncle Vito. It serves as the family meeting place. But we try not to make that public. So we walked in the front door this time, just like normal restaurant patrons. It was uncommonly quiet inside.

Dino took off his sunglasses the way that detective in *CSI Miami* does. I let my eyes adjust to the dark. The place was empty except for Kitty. She was seated by herself at a table near the back, drinking an espresso.

Of course there was a white tablecloth on the table. This was a class joint.

Kitty grinned and waved us over. "*Ciao*, Del. Dino."

I leaned down for my usual two-cheek kisses. Her face was a road map of wrinkles, the skin soft and powdery. Her once-dark hair had advanced from gray to pure white. But the brown eyes were as sharp as ever.

We slid into chairs opposite her. She got right to the point. "You two know what I mean when I say *The A-Team*?"

Dino squinted. "That TV show from the eighties? The one about the Vietnam vets who became vigilantes?"

"That's the one." She leaned forward. Her dark eyes gleamed. "They're a bunch of old guys now. Retired. So I'm starting a new one."

"New TV show?" I asked, perplexed. Surely she knew the A-Team wasn't real.

"Nope. Vigilante group. I talked to your mom. We need one, with all the senior scams these days." She leaned back in the chair and looked off into the distance with a spooky smile. "I'm thinking of calling it...the B-Team. And Del, we want you to run it."

My brother groaned.

• • •

That was five months ago. A whole lot has happened since then.

There are four of us vigilantes now. Me, Dino, Kitty and Ritz. Hard to describe my old pal from high school. Her real name is Rita, but we call her Ritz, after the crackers. Big hint there. Remember Murdock from *The A-Team*? Back in the politically incorrect days of the eighties, he would have been what we called "certified crazy." Ritz is not far off that.

We operate from an empty house in Hamilton. Kitty has a small supply of them. She calls this her "two-story pension plan." Clever idea to park her laundered earnings in real estate. Mom helped her with financial planning. When Kitty needs money to fund our operations, she simply sells another house.

I remember very clearly how this particular job got started. It was a Saturday afternoon, which explained why I could be there. I have a different job during the week. Kitty and Ritz covered the office Monday to Friday. Ritz had wandered in earlier, looking for company. When the phone rang she grabbed it and answered in her characteristic gruff manner.

"B-Team. Make it snappy. We're busy."

I grimaced. Yes, you had to be tough, being female in this game. That's Ritz. Pure rawhide.

As she said on the phone, we're the B-Team. We deal in justice, not the law. Sometimes the law lets you down. We try to rectify that.

Ritz turned to me. "It's Kitty. She wants to talk to you."

I grabbed the receiver from her hand before she shoved it in my face. Ritz is a tad abrupt.

"Yup," I said into the phone.

"Still on for tonight?" Kitty's voice was

businesslike. She knew I wasn't happy about this job.

"Yeah. Sure." I wasn't the type to back out.

"Del, are you sure about Ritz? This is a tricky one."

I looked over at the person in question. Ritz was cleaning her fingernails with the corner of a business card.

"I'm never sure about Ritz," I muttered into the phone.

Kitty rang off.

Ritz turned to me. Her dark, beady eyes were a stark contrast to her flaxen curls.

"You don't need me until tonight." It was a statement.

I shook my head. Ritz is our weapons gal. There is nothing she doesn't know about hardware and tearing things apart. I like to tease her about the tools she carries. Ritz has screwdrivers where other women carry lipstick.

"Then I'll be at the range." Ritz lifted her squat body from the beat-up office chair. She grabbed her backpack from the floor and sauntered to the door. "See you tonight."

A few weeks ago, I asked Ritz why she risked her freedom doing vigilante jobs with us. *I hate it when innocent people get crapped on by scumbags* was her answer.

Can't argue with that. I got an uneasy feeling as I watched her leave.

TWO

At seven that night, we had a final conference call over the Internet.

Dino was on the line from New York. His handsome cherub face filled the screen. "I cased the joint earlier this week. No alarm system in evidence or on record. Second-floor windows left open."

Kitty said, "They're going to Vegas for the weekend."

"How do you know that?" Dino said.

"We have the same cleaning people," said Kitty. "They talk to me."

Everyone talks to Kitty. Such a sweet little old lady. She could charm the sharks in the sea, let alone the ones on land.

If they only knew her like we do...

"What's the backstory?" asked Ritz. Her pug face dominated the screen.

It took me a moment to remember that Ritz hadn't been in on the first meeting for this job. Without the background, she didn't know the reason we were doing it.

"We're working for wife number one," said Kitty. "Angela. Recently divorced, not her idea. We're after a diamond necklace that belongs to her. The new wife has been swanning around town, wearing it like a big trophy. It isn't hers to wear. Angela wants it back."

I couldn't keep my mouth shut. "This isn't exactly a hard-luck story."

"Del, we've discussed this." Her voice was impatient. "The necklace was given to Angela by her grandmother. Not her ex."

"I'm not so thrilled about risking my butt for rich people." I mean, this wasn't exactly Robin Hood material. Usually, we helped people who had been preyed upon by heartless bastards.

"Angela isn't rich. The lawyers got rich. You know how it goes."

I still grumbled.

"Okay, how do the rest of you feel? Do you want to pull out?" Kitty asked.

"I don't really count since I'm not there to be part of it," said Dino.

"Ritz?"

"Nah. It's a job. I like jobs," said Ritz.

Typical response from Ritz. It made me shiver.

"Del?"

I sighed. "I'll do it if Ritz does. But I hope

our next job is a little more in line with our mandate."

"You just don't understand, Del."

"You're right. I don't."

"We don't discriminate against people based on income or anything else. If they've been done wrong, we step in. Simple as that."

"Yeah, yeah. I hear you." What she said was true. Kitty set the rules. Kitty set us up in this business to begin with, and she paid our expenses. It's her baby. I figure it's her way of making a bid for heaven after a somewhat questionable early career.

Our mission is to help the underdog. That is, people who have been on the losing side of a bad deal and will likely suffer greatly because of it. Our most recent cases involved restoring someone's good name, and preventing a blackmailer from preying on the helpless. Both noble endeavors.

This divorcee was hardly an underdog,

and helping her get back an heirloom diamond necklace was not the sort of thing I like to take risks for.

But I thought the world of Kitty. And if Kitty wanted to do this, I would swallow my feelings and do it.

"See you at midnight," I said.

THREE

Chapter seven in the book *Burglary for Dummies* states, *Always double-check your intelligence.* (*Burglary for Dummies* was written by my cousin Gina and is available through most book retailers.)

I didn't know who was in Vegas, because the master bedroom at 224 Lakeshore Road was clearly occupied this night.

Metallic squeals, repeated frequently. That would be bedsprings.

Oomphs and moans. That would be obvious.

I backed away from the doorway and tiptoed down the hall to the guest bedroom. Once there, I took the cell phone from my black leather waist pouch.

Mission aborted, I texted into the phone.

Crap, typed the body at the other end. **Ready for pickup**.

I clicked off and put the cell away.

Well, that had been a total waste of effort.

The night was dark, with only a quarter moon punctuating the sky. The air was cold for late October. I hoofed it to the window and turned around. Then I climbed swiftly down the heavy Boston ivy until both hands were holding on to the windowsill. It was only a short drop to the ground from there.

I'm long and lean, like my brother, and pretty athletic. So it didn't occur to me that anything could go wrong.

I let go of the sill.

A second later my feet were on solid ground and I was down in a crouch. Perfect landing. I straightened up.

Strong arms reached around me from behind. I froze.

"That's not an elbow you're holding on to," I said indignantly.

"Whoops," said a low male voice. "Sorry about that." The hands shifted down to my waist, where they held on hard.

Sorry? A polite assailant?

Both of my arms were trapped. I could feel my butt pressed into a really warm and solid form.

"Keep quiet or I'll raise an alarm." The voice was definitely male.

So not an assailant. A cop? Security guard?

"Did you steal anything?" That voice again, in my left ear.

I shook my head carefully. It was even true. I hadn't. This was because I couldn't get into the room where the damn necklace was located.

The man snorted. “You’re dressed all in black and climbing out a window. What else could you be doing?”

“Having an affair?” I whispered cheerfully. “Nope, not me. I’m pure as the driven snow. You want to talk to the two going at it in there. ”

“You’re kidding,” uttered the voice. It didn’t sound particularly surprised or upset.

Ritz, where the hell are you? Move to plan B, dammit.

The hold on me loosened. I turned around in the man’s arms.

For a moment a cloud passed over the moon, and the night shrouded us. My eyes needed to adjust to the low light. The man who stared back at me was about my age. Dark brown curly hair, brown eyes, crooked nose that looked as if it had been broken more than once. But there was no disguising the muscle in the arms that held me firmly, nor the rugged planes of his face. Or the eyebrows that swooped into a frown.

"Hey, I *know* you," he said. The dark eyes went wide.

I froze. Memories of high school danced in my head. Football. A souped-up Camaro. A botched attempt at backseat seduction. Dino getting into a fight with the guy staring down at me now. My older cousins breaking it up. Me sneaking away before the lecture started...

I never could resist a fast car.

Crap! I knew who he was. Mac, Mac... what was his name?

This was *so* not part of the plan.

"Who are you?" he whispered. Man, that voice was sexy. His big hands locked on my upper arms.

I looked him in the eyes then. I tried to look sad and sincere.

"I'm sorry," I said mournfully. "I really am." And I would have been. It was only out of sheer necessity that I was going to knee him in the crotch.

The stream of freezing water came out of nowhere and hit us both.

"Shit!" I shrieked. "Holy freakin' hell! *Ritz*!!" This wasn't part of the plan either.

"Son of a—" (*sputter, gasp, spit*).

She moved the blast from him and me to him, and he took it right in the face. The big hands released me. I leaped back out of reach as the poor guy started gagging.

"Move away from him, Del!"

I stumbled farther back.

Ritz dropped the hose, ran forward and lifted her right arm.

Whomp.

I watched in horror as the poor guy crumpled.

"Run!" yelled Ritz.

I didn't run. The only thing that moved

was my head. I stared down at the man on the ground. He didn't move.

I was soaked, and it suddenly got colder out. "Is he dead?" I croaked.

"Nah. Just out of commission for a while." Ritz was a whiz at martial arts. Which didn't exactly jibe with her appearance. Imagine a pint-sized Brunhilda.

I peered down at her victim's face. It looked serene. Innocent and serene. Sort of...sweet. Like a little boy having a dream.

"You gave him quite a whack there."

Ritz shrugged. "I do my best."

I touched him with the tip of my toe. He didn't move.

"Come on," she said.

"We can't just leave him here. He's hurt." Not to mention we were the ones who had hurt him.

"We gotta get out of here," she insisted.

"Ritz, we can't. He's out cold." The poor

guy looked so vulnerable. "Anything could happen to him. Coyotes could eat him."

"Coyotes? In the middle of the city?"

"I've seen them at the animal shelter, hanging around. You know there are coyotes in the ravines. Lots of them. It's been all over the news."

"You're getting soft, Del. You know that? Why do you care? What's this guy to you?"

I thought for a sec. Was I getting soft? He was my assailant. But as assailants go, he was a pretty nice one. After all, he did apologize for grabbing me where he shouldn't.

"He's unconscious. Defenseless. I just can't leave the poor fellow to be eaten."

"Oh no. Don't make this dude your latest project, Del."

That annoyed me. "What do you mean?"

"Your latest lame duck! Wounded bird." She flung her arms up. "You're always rescuing something."

"I'm not rescuing him! I'm just..." What? What was I?

"What was the guy doing here anyway? Lurking around like that. Have you thought about it?" she said.

I hesitated. "Maybe he's one of us?"

"One of us," parroted Ritz. "One of us like a vigilante? Or one of us like a bad-guy burglar?"

Hell, I didn't know.

"Don't go all sentimental on me, Del. We haven't got the time."

"I'm not sentimental!" I protested vigorously. "I'm not."

Ritz was pacing now. "You're friggin' loony. We can't stand out here debating the issue. What do you propose?"

I looked across the manicured front lawn of this enormous home. Even in the dark, I could see the carefully trimmed shrubbery and cedars. Lots of places for wild animals to hide.

"We need to get him inside somewhere. Where he won't be eaten."

Ritz stopped pacing and crossed her arms. "The doors to the house are all locked. I checked while you were climbing in."

Damn. That would mean I'd have to climb the ivy and go through the window again, sneak down the stairs without anyone hearing, and open a door from the inside. Could we get him inside without the lovebirds hearing?

More important, if they heard us, would they call the cops? I was allergic to cops.

This wasn't a good plan. But I just couldn't leave him here.

The water was starting to freeze on me. I shivered.

"Hurry and make up your mind," said Ritz, stomping her feet in the slick grass. "It's cold out here."

There was only one thing to do. And Ritz wasn't going to like it one bit.

"Help me," I said. "Help me move him to the front door."

"*What!*"

"Here, grab his feet." Maybe if I just gave her orders, she wouldn't think about it. It worked sometimes.

"Are you crazy?"

I hesitated. Okay, yes, this was nuts. We were on a job. A totally screwed-up job, admittedly, but still. It didn't allow for side trips.

Not to mention the poor guy probably wouldn't appreciate being moved right now.

I struggled for a reasonable answer. "We'll move him to the front door. Then I'll ring the doorbell a zillion times to make sure they come down to check it out."

The cursing started then. Ritz can curse like a Russian seaman.

"Grab his feet," I said.

"One day, Del, your soft side is going to

land us in jail," she muttered. "You take his feet. I'm stronger. I'll take his shoulders."

I discovered something. It's not so easy to tuck a man's leg under your arm and then reach down to grab the other leg without falling over. Two hundred pounds of dead weight is heavier than it sounds.

We shuffled our way toward the massive front steps and stopped on the grass to the right of them. With a grunt Ritz dropped her end of the load on the ground. She wasn't too gentle about it.

"That's it," said Ritz. "No way we can get him up those steps without banging his head."

I considered the situation. She was right about the steps.

Besides, I had an idea. Anyone opening the door would see a dead or sleeping body at the bottom of the steps. They might think he'd hurt himself falling down the stairs. Hey. That made me feel better.

"Okay, just help me move him to the bottom of the stairs then."

Ritz picked up his shoulders and dragged him to the flagstone walk. I made sure his head landed gently this time.

"Now what?" asked Ritz.

I launched myself up the stairs and rang the doorbell. I did that about ten times and then switched to pounding on the door.

"Move it," said Ritz behind me. "They just turned on the lights upstairs. Let's get out of here."

I fled down the stairs and stopped at the bottom for one last look at our victim. His eyes were shut, but he was making little moaning sounds now.

"Sorry," I said to the poor guy. He didn't answer back.

FOUR

We ran as if ravenous zombies were after us. Sounds of moaning and then coughing retreated in the distance.

Ritz managed to keep up with me. This always surprised me, as she doesn't really have the body for it.

And right now I wanted to kill her, I was so drenched. Lucky for her, there was no time for that. I didn't stop running until we reached the car.

Kitty was waiting down the road and around the corner in her old Jeep. The passenger door was open. Kitty was a pro.

I slipped into the front seat and pulled the door shut. Ritz tumbled into the back, and Kitty pulled away from the curb.

Now that I had stopped running and rescuing people from coyotes, the cold set in.

"Holy shit, Ritz! I'm freezing!"

"I improvised. Worked, didn't it?" Ritz was cool, as usual.

"Turn up the heat, will you, Kitty?"

She turned up the heat.

"My heart is beating triple time. I can't tell if I'm panting from running or shivering to death. Jeesh, that water was cold."

"Someone was there?" Kitty said.

"Not only that, but someone was waiting for me outside," I said. "Why the hell didn't you signal me, Ritz? You were supposed to be on watch."

"I didn't see the dude, obviously."

Kitty cursed and shifted gears. "But you got away okay. I take it Ritz found a hose?"

"Yeah. I flooded the bastard. And then I whomped him good."

I could hear the grin in her voice. Really, sometimes Ritz scares the crap out of me.

I was still feeling guilty about the dude we had left behind. He didn't seem like a bad guy. But really. Serves him right. What the heck was he doing lurking outside the house? He was obviously up to something.

We whizzed along Lakeshore, past Bronte Road and Burloak Drive. Kitty was quiet, seemingly deep in thought.

"Sorry, Del. I was sure they were away this weekend."

"Oh, I expect one of them is in Vegas, all right. Just as I equally suspect the other is not."

Kitty whistled low. "You think he's cheating on her?"

"More likely her on him. Our client might get a kick out of that. Maybe that will be some recompense. We still don't have the necklace."

Kitty smiled as we drove past Appleby. "That's okay. I have another plan."

I groaned.

Great-Aunt Kitty is my grandmother's much younger sister. Grandma was the oldest of thirteen, may she rest in peace. Kitty is the youngest, which puts her at seventysome-thing. She never had kids, so my parents made her my godmother.

Good thing I am fond of Kitty. It's hard to avoid your godmother in an Italian family. Let me put it this way: the extended family I try to avoid is well known in Steeltown. You might say they run the place. That is, when they aren't in the slammer doing time.

I make a point of not associating with most of them. I still keep in touch with my cousin Gina, who is closer to the family than I am but similarly allergic. Gina is engaged to Pete, a really great guy who used to play pro football. I haven't done so well in the marriage department. Sadly, my choices in men have sucked. I am a total loser when it comes to relationships.

Kitty's house was coming into view now. She pulled into the secluded laneway. My car was there where I'd left it.

"Come on, Ritz," I said. "I'll drive you home." We both got out of the Jeep. I had my keys out. I was almost to my car when Kitty's voice rang out behind me.

"Hold on a minute, Del. I want to talk to you." She slammed the Jeep door behind her.

I turned to face her. All five feet of her.

"Look. I know what you're thinking. I can see it on your face," she said.

"Aunt Kitty, I'm soaking wet, freezing my butt off. We got a man out cold from a

Ritz-attack, and we just a botched a burglary. Give me one reason why I should risk my butt again for a pretty necklace." I wrapped both arms around my chest to keep warm.

"Listen to me, Del! Take a second to imagine what it must be like." She waved a hand through the air at me. "You have a husband, a home, kids, a nice lifestyle. You probably gave up a good career to make it all happen. Then all of a sudden, you're turfed out of your own life. And the husband? He doesn't lose a thing."

She was pacing now, throwing her arms around like a true Italian. "It's like your whole world goes on without you, with some upstart actress playing your role. And you're left watching helplessly from the sidelines."

I stared at her, coming out of my trance. Holy crap, this wasn't about our client. This was much more personal. I'd never known Kitty's husband, but it was common knowledge that he'd taken off with some younger woman a million years ago. The family still talked about it. He'd left without getting a divorce, which meant Kitty couldn't remarry.

I got it. This was about getting revenge for all women who had been sucker punched by losers.

Kitty stopped and turned to me. The persuasive voice kicked up a notch. "The thing is, Angela has done *nothing wrong*. And yet *her* life is turned upside down, and the life of her cheating husband hardly changes at all. It's horribly unfair, and we're all about fighting inequity, aren't we? I mean, that's what the B-Team is about. Righting the wrongs that happen to people who don't deserve such treatment."

She had me at that, and she knew it. But even so, she had to sweeten the pot.

"You know what it's like to be let down by men. Just as much as I do."

She was referring to ex-fiancé number two.

"Okay, you win," I said, unlocking my car door with a click. "But sometimes I wish Stella hadn't volunteered me for this team."

"Do you, Del? Do you really?"

Damn. She had me again. No, I didn't.

Stella is my mother.

FIVE

For years I have toyed with the idea of writing a book. I even have a title for it—*My Mother's in the Mob.*

Stella Scarlotti was born on a cold day in January 1952. The men in the family said that ice had formed in her heart the day she was born. I knew different.

It wasn't ice. It was steel. This is an industrial city, after all. And so, from the very beginning, Stella has taken no crap. Not from anyone.

Besides having eyes that can cut right through you, Stella has another talent. She is great with numbers. And so she became the family accountant. You want to know where the money is, Stella knows. She can also tell you where the bodies are buried. Which is one of the reasons you don't want to get on her bad side. People tiptoe around Stella.

Stella wasn't a bad mom. It's just that she knew every bad thing I was doing before I even thought of doing it.

About five years ago something happened that tempered her heart. Dad crashed his vintage Alfa Romeo on the Burlington Bay Skyway. He drives a big late-model convertible for the angels now. I imagine them all piling in, singing "Stairway to Heaven" at the top of their lungs.

After Dad died, Mom started getting angry about the injustices in the world.

Then a friend of Kitty's was taken to the cleaners by a so-called suitor. Mom told Kitty to go to me, because Stella knew I couldn't resist a challenge like this. She was dead right. We've been serving the cause of justice ever since. Justice for those who won't get it any other way.

•••

Dino called at seven the next evening, as planned. I was just getting into my car for the meeting.

"Did you see the billboard?" He sounded all excited.

"I saw the billboard," I said, with a smile in my voice. "I even took a photo of it—that's how good a sister I am. Check your email."

"Thanks, Del. Tony says it's going up in LA next week." Tony was Dino's modeling agent.

It was nice to hear Dino so happy. So I wasn't prepared for the next line.

"Thing is, Del, I have to stay in New York until next week."

"*What!*"

"The advertising brass from Kilty Boys Underwear. They're coming into town and want to meet me."

"Dammit, Dino! We need you."

Pause. "I'm sorry, Del. But if you knew how important this is...I just can't miss it. It could mean Europe. Mom's flying here to deal with the negotiations."

He went on, but I was only half listening. This was Dino, through and through. Really sweet, and with a face as cute as an Italian cherub. Kind to cats and dogs and old people. But unreliable. Something always came up with Dino, even when we were kids. Worse, it was "never his fault."

And truly, it wasn't. You know how some

people are bad luck, and you can't explain it? It's like that, only Dino is bad luck for other people. Usually me.

"Can't you postpone the job until I get back?" he said.

I grumbled some more. "I'll talk to the others."

I clicked off feeling frustrated.

Yeah, we could postpone. But when would we ever have an opportunity like this again?

It took me ten minutes to drive from my place to Kitty's. I was already in a foul mood. So I let my mind go back to Kitty's comment about ex-fiancé number two.

Yes, one man shouldn't color your whole opinion of mankind in general. And there was no question I had been stalling on the lover front. It had been over a year since I'd whacked the dirtbag in my life across the face with my swanky Kate Spade handbag. (Handbag was toast, but it was totally worth it.)

Kitty was right. Damned if I was going to let one disloyal jerk affect the rest of my life. I was a big girl. I controlled my own future. Starting right now, I was going to get out there and try to find loser number three.

I was still ruminating on where to meet him when I pulled up in front of Kitty's little place in the woods. Ritz was already there, I could see. Her motorcycle was parked close to the garage. I let myself into the foyer and threw my purse down on the tufted hall bench.

"We're in the kitchen," yelled Kitty from down the hall.

I made my way to the bright, white kitchen. Ritz was already sitting on a black-and-chrome bar stool. I nodded to her and then turned my head to Kitty. As usual, one look and I had to smile. Kitty may look like a small, fluffy senior, but she's razor sharp, and she knows how to dress.

"Dino can't make it back in time," I reported.

Kitty had a wineglass in one hand and a bottle in the other. She stopped mid-pour.

"Shit," she said. She finished pouring and handed me a glass. "You'll need this."

"Don't need Dino," said Ritz.

"I don't know who else we could get," Kitty said. "Everyone else will be at the event."

"You deaf?" Ritz had a voice full of gravel. "I don't need anyone else."

I swung my gaze to her. "No lookout, Ritz. You okay with that?"

"Piece of cake." Ritz looked at us with crazy eyes.

I didn't know whether to groan now or wait until she spilled the words.

"Those rich peeps are going to the Black Cat gig on Thursday, right?"

I nodded.

"So I break in while they're there. Like we planned."

Now I groaned. "Ritz, we can't help you. I'm running the event. Kitty and I have to be there."

She shrugged. "So? Like I haven't done jobs on my own before!"

What? What jobs? "Wait a minute. I didn't know you'd—"

"Nothing to worry about," Kitty said quickly. "All in the past."

"But—"

"Can it," said Ritz. "You don't want to know."

My eyes shifted between them. Ritz had turned away from me. Kitty was studying the wine in her glass. Did I want to know? Okay, maybe not. Still, it was hard not to be pissed off. What else didn't I know?

"So what are you thinking, Ritz?" Kitty asked. She took a swig from the crystal glass.

Ritz shrugged. "Same MO as last time.

I can climb as good as Del here. Know the right window. Easy."

I frowned. That particular MO hadn't worked very well. "Except what if that same guy is still casing the joint?"

Ritz looked at me with disgust. "Not stupid. I'll do the ground surveillance. Now that we know. We didn't know before."

"She has a point, Del," said Kitty. "But who will be your getaway driver?"

"I'll use the bike."

Ritz had a late-model Ducati. Probably a fighter jet couldn't catch up to her.

"So it's settled," said Kitty. "Ritz will break into the house while we keep the owners busy at the charity gala."

Settled. *Right.* Which was more than I could say for my stomach.

We drank the rest of the wine. It didn't help with the stomach. When we wrapped up the business meeting, Kitty suggested

I stay behind to discuss last-minute gala details. As soon as Ritz left, I blurted out my misgivings.

"Sometimes that girl scares the crap out of me," I said.

Kitty cocked her head. Her fluffy hair bobbed. "Strange thing. Seeing as you are the one she looks up to and tries to copy."

That startled me. "What are you talking about?"

"Come on, Del. Ritz followed you around like a grumpy puppy all through school."

More like a leech attached to my leg. But I didn't say that out loud.

"Ever since you pulled off that caper with the nuns, you had her undying devotion."

"Oh *that*," I said. "I didn't actually mean for the fire trucks to come. I just sort of got carried away."

"It doesn't matter," said Kitty, poking a stubby finger in my direction. "You saved her bacon—and did it in such a way that no one ever figured it out. What's more, you never boasted about it. That's the sort of class Ritz admires."

I harrumphed and shifted my butt on the bar stool. *Class*. Don't think I've ever heard that word and my name in the same sentence. *Class* is not what gets you suspended from school, if you get my drift.

I thought about Ritz on the drive home. My uncomfortable feeling of doom came down to one question. Why did I distrust Ritz to pull off this heist on her own?

Was it me? Was I harboring a control issue? Usually I was the mastermind of every job we did. That's the way it had worked in the past. And usually those jobs came off without a hitch.

Okay, there was that one unfortunate incident with the Chihuahua and the stripper. But truly, that was an anomaly. He looked like a woman from a distance. Almost anyone could have made that mistake.

So why was I nervous about this necklace heist? It was weird. Something about it didn't feel right to me. Couldn't for the life of me figure out what.

But Kitty was keen, and I cared a lot about Kitty. She was the best relative a girl could have. She'd held my hand and taken away the gun when my last fiancé cheated on me. Then she grabbed my arm when I was about to throw the ring off the Burlington Skyway bridge.

"Be smart," she had insisted, prying the emerald-cut diamond from my fist. "It drives them crazy when you sell their rings for 10 percent of what they paid."

Kitty was a pro, all right. And if Kitty wanted to see this through, I would tromp along at her side, fighting off alligators till the very end.

Ritz was a different story. I didn't think she was caught up much in the moral or philosophical issues of what we did. That girl just liked danger. And even if I was de facto the leader of this pack, Ritz was the only one of us who was truly badass.

Enough of being mother. I was simply going to have to let the badass kid do the job on her own.

SiX

About the Black Cat gig...

Most of the stuff we do as the B-Team is night work. This is a good thing, because I actually have a day job. Believe it or not, it involves cats. And dogs. And thc occasional rabbit or ferret.

I work for the local animal shelter. I'm their event planner and fundraising coordinator. Kitty is on the board of directors. She is also a major sponsor of the shelter. All of us who work there help care for our beloved animals until they are adopted. But it takes more than love and affection to support the animals that find their way to our shelter. It takes money. And money is where I come in.

The Black Cat Masquerade is our biggest fundraiser of the year. It's also *the* place for the glitterati to be seen. Partygoers dress to the nines and pay a nice ticket price to attend the event. The mayor comes, and so do television personalities who live locally. Everyone wears masks.

This year the event was being held in Paloma Mansion, down on the lake. It's a gorgeous 1920s mansion that was previously owned by a long-ago relative of dubious repute. He willed it to the town. I come from a long line of dubious relatives trying to buy their way into that big angel fest in the sky.

It was Thursday night. My event team was in place, and the band Soulidified was playing soul music. I watched from the huge foyer as Mercedes and BMWs dumped their passengers off at the end of the circular driveway.

My pintsized assistant, Alison, stepped up to my side. "The decor is brilliant," she said. "Everyone says so."

I gazed around at the paintings of sparkly masks that lined the hall. The glittery masked-ball theme continued throughout the main ballroom and upstairs to the silent-auction room. Candlelight washed the walls with a romantic glow. Mirrored vases reflected the shimmering silver fabric that topped the tables. The whole effect was one big *wow*.

"We've sold out," said Alison. She beamed with excitement. "It's going to be a huge success, Del. You'll see."

"Cross your fingers," I said. It was expensive to put on these sorts of events. A lot like a posh wedding. Much of our success depended on the money raised by the silent auction. We had received donated gifts from stores and businesses in town. With luck, the people who came tonight would bid generously on those items. Our shelter animals depended on it.

I put on my biggest smile and did the welcoming-hostess thing for the next half-hour. I shook hands with a television personality from the Weather Network. Also with the mayor and his wife. I even got to see the evil woman at the center of our current job—Cindy Morton, wife number two, in the flesh. She was on the arm of her rich, older husband, wearing a cut-to-there gown. I kept my eye on her from a distance. If they started to leave, I would think of a reason to keep them here.

Servers were bringing out the mini beef Wellingtons and shrimp tempura. I had just climbed the stairs to the auction room when my cell phone vibrated.

I glanced down at the text. It was from Ritz.

Problem call me

Call her? On a cell phone? While she was in the middle of a heist? What the hell was going on?

I texted back, **ok**.

Then I turned to Alison. "I have to run outside to make a phone call. It's too noisy in here."

She nodded. "Go," she said.

I didn't waste time. I made my way through the crowd, smiling at everyone but definitely showing I was in a hurry. Down the stairs I raced, then into the front hall and out the double doors to the circular drive, where the drivers of several posh cars waited patiently for their owners.

I passed people smoking on the steps, gave them a cheery nod and then moved off far enough to get some privacy.

Ritz answered on the first ring.

"You wanna get over here," she said.

Okay, so she wasn't dying. This wasn't an emergency. I went from anxious to pissed in one second flat. I do that a lot where Ritz is concerned.

"Ritz, I'm right in the middle of the event! I can't leave."

"Get here. Find a way." She clicked off.

What the hell? I stared at the phone in my hand. Then I swore and dialed again.

"Why me? Why not Kitty?"

"You'll see when you get here. Just do it."

Click.

Once again I was left staring at the phone in my hand.

Damn that Ritz. Why did I let her boss me around like this?

Leave now? Okay, I could put Alison in charge of operations, and get Kitty to cover for me in the PR department. It would only take me five minutes to get there. Five there, five back and hopefully only five with Ritz. I could always say I had to run back to the office for something.

I slipped back into the mansion, gave commands to both Alison and Kitty, and ran out with my purse.

The Mustang was parked around the back. I got in and started her up. I wasted no time pulling onto the driveway and passed several cars coming in.

All the way there, I was thinking madly. Ritz said there was a "problem." What could be the problem? If it was cops, she would have said so.

Coyotes? Did she run into a coyote? But then, why me? Why ever would she need me specifically?

I turned into the familiar driveway. The house was mainly in darkness, except for a dim light coming from one of the far rooms. As soon as I got out of the car, I texted Ritz.

I'm here.

Then I waited.

House next door. Left side. Kitchen.

More bafflement on my part. Why was she next door?

I left the car and walked across the grassy expanse to the house on the left. It was equally big, although not as in-your-face about it.

Kitchen. Ritz had said *kitchen*. I assumed that meant she was in there, and I didn't need to be careful or anything. Still, I tried not to draw attention to myself. No one had turned on the outdoor lighting, so the front of the house was dark. I moved swiftly up to the double front doors. One was unlocked. I pushed it open and made my way quietly down the dark hall to where the light originated.

Ritz *was* in the kitchen. I could see her as I approached the doorway. She sat on a bar stool at the solid-oak kitchen island, swinging her short legs. "Want a beer?" she said, holding a brew up with one hand for me to see.

I stared at her. She pointed to the other person sitting at the end of the island.

"Holy crap on a stick," I said.

SEVEN

The man across from me looked a lot like the guy Ritz had whomped when we botched the first burglary. You might even say he was one and the same. I stared at him. He nodded at me. Then he took a swig from his beer bottle.

That freaked me out even more.

I swung my gaze back to Ritz. "This had better be good, Ritz," I said.

She gestured at the counter.

I looked down on the black granite in front of me. Particularly at the gun resting nicely on it.

"Walther," I said absently. "Not one of ours." In the family, we own Glocks. A much superior weapon.

"Nope," said Ritz. "So here's the thing. This is Canada, not Jersey. Give it a thought. Why would this dude be carrying?"

"I'm all ears," I said. "Why don't you ask him? He's sitting to the left of you, for some unfathomable reason."

Why wasn't anyone telling me what was going on?

"Call me Mac," he said.

"Is that your name? Or do you just like to be called that?"

A thin grin stretched across his face. It didn't reach his hard brown eyes. "Short for MacQuarrie. Like you don't already know." He leaned back and gave me the once-over.

"You're all grown up now, Red. It looks good on you."

I frowned. "You really want to open with that line? 'Cause I'm still on good terms with my brother and cousins."

Mac looked thoughtful. "So you do remember me."

"You don't forget your first clumsy grope," I said.

He snorted. "I didn't forget you either. Your brother gave me something to remember you by." He pointed to his nose. Which wasn't straight.

I repeated his words. "Looks good on you."

Now he laughed. It was a deep, throaty laugh, far too attractive.

"I forgot about your sassy mouth, Red."

My hair isn't red. It's auburn. No one has called me Red in years. It made me feel...sort of weird. Not sure if in a good way or bad.

"What's with the cat-suit getup?" he said.

"Fundraiser. Ritz pulled me out of a gala I was running. And where I should be right now."

He nodded. "Of course. The Black Cat Masquerade. I saw it advertised. You look good in a cat suit. Turn around."

I gave him the finger.

He laughed out loud.

Ritz finally went to the fridge and came back with my beer. She handed it to me.

"Uh, Ritz..." I handed it back to her. She made a grunting sound as she twisted the screw cap off. She shoved it back at me.

"Thanks," I said.

Mac watched this display. He seemed thoroughly amused.

"So I have tender hands," I said. I took a swig, swallowed and continued. "Balances out my hard heart."

Ritz snorted this time. "You, hard? You're the one who had to save this dude from being eaten by coyotes."

"Coyotes?" Mac said. "In the city?"

I cut in before this degenerated into something maudlin.

"Well, this has been lovely, but now I have to scream. Will someone please tell me why we're all sitting around this kitchen?" This very nice kitchen. In a very nice but totally strange house.

"He's okay, Del," said Ritz. "He actually does work for Stella."

Mom? I nearly dropped the bottle. "Are you freaking kidding me?"

"And he knows Uncle Vince."

I took a swig from the bottle and kept going. I didn't stop until it was half empty. Then I lowered the bottle and wiped my mouth with the side of my hand. "Explain," I said hoarsely. "Before I go nuts."

"This may take some time," he said.

I stared at him until my eyes went blurry. "Are you security or something? What exactly *were* you doing next door that night we tried to burgle the place?"

Even more to the point, what was he doing here *now*? In fact, why were we in the house next door *at all*?

"Security," said Mac. "Most definitely. But not the other night."

"Crap," I muttered. This wasn't going to be good.

Ritz snorted like a pug. "Wait for it."

Mac leaned back on the stool. "Simple, really. My parents live in this house. They're up north for a week. I'm staying here to look after the place. I like to walk at night. I was just coming back when I saw you climb out of that window next door."

I gave a low whistle. "So that's why you were out front."

Mac grinned again. It reminded me of a devilish kid. "Could have knocked me out with a marshmallow when you came climbing down that ivy. The woman next door has a loose reputation, according to my mother. Then I saw you. And you were most definitely a babe and a half. Were you visiting Cindy in the night? Is Cindy a lesbian? With her rep with men?"

Ritz made that pug sound again. "Too funny. Especially with *your* rep."

"Can it," I warned Ritz. Jeesh, that was all I needed right now. A regaling of my stupid relationships with men.

I glared at her. "So what did you tell him?"

"The truth," she said. That didn't help me. I didn't know whether she was saying that to convince him or if she really *had* told him the truth.

Luckily, she continued. "I told him we were retrieving a necklace that belonged to the first wife. A necklace that had been given to her by her grandmother. This one, in fact." She reached into her pocket and held up something that blinded me with sparkle.

Crap! Ritz had the necklace. And she had told Mac the truth. Which meant—

"I was waiting for her when she came out of the house tonight," Mac explained. He seemed to be reading my mind.

All very nice, but where exactly did we stand now? Was Mac going to let us go scot-free?

"You know Stonehouse Security?" he said.

"I've heard of it," I said. Of course I had. It was state of the art in the biz. My uncles used Stonehouse to secure our warehouses and other operations.

Ritz pointed a thumb at Mac. "That's Stonehouse. In the flesh."

My jaw dropped.

"My uncle started it. I recently took over when he retired," said Mac.

"So your uncle's name is Stonehouse?" I had to ask.

"No, it's MacQuarrie, like mine. Quarry. Get it?"

I groaned. Stonehouse. Stones are mined from a quarry. Somebody had a wicked sense of humor.

"And I expect your little job tonight will garner me a new client tomorrow," said Mac.

Ritz grinned. "Hey! You should hire us. We break into houses. You can sell the owners better security after."

"Ritz," I growled.

"We should get a commission," said Ritz. She hooted like an asthmatic donkey.

"Out!" I said to her. "*Now.*" I put my beer bottle on the counter and stood up. I turned to Mac. "This has been very nice, but I really have to return to the gala I am running. Thank you for your hospitality. And your understanding. I hope we can return the favor someday."

He lifted his bottle in salute.

I really hoped he was going to be understanding. I also hoped I didn't have to return the favor. But what I really wanted was to get out of there before he called the police.

I turned tail and made fast tracks back to the gala.

EIGHT

He didn't call the police. Ritz and I remained unmolested by the boys in blue.

I thought a lot about that over my coffee the next morning. Was Mac a supporter of vigilante justice, like I was? Did he approve of our trying to help people, even if it meant stepping outside the law a wee bit to do so?

Or was his motive for keeping his mouth shut merely financial? If Mac was Stonehouse Security, then he had a lucrative client in my extended family. Probably it would be in his financial interest not to report us.

Whatever the reason, I was relieved. But still wary.

I spent the morning doing cleanup from the gala. It had been a great success but a lot of work. You wouldn't believe how much has to be done after a big event. Decorations have to be stored. Bills have to be paid. Checks and cash from the silent auction have to be tallied. I worked hard with Alison in the office all day while our animal-care workers took care of the kennels.

The following day Ritz and I had an appointment. Our client, Angela Morton, was arriving to pick up the necklace.

We converged at Kitty's place shortly after noon. Ritz pulled her Ducati up behind my red Mustang. A late-model Merc sat in the driveway as well. It had to be the client's.

I got out of the car and turned to Ritz,

who was taking off her helmet. "Nice wheels for a poor divorcee," I said.

Ritz shrugged. "Probably got it in the settlement." She strapped her helmet to the bike and took out her smartphone. I could see she was setting up to take a photo of the house. Ritz was camera-mad.

"Don't. Kitty doesn't like anyone taking photos of her place," I warned. "She stays under the radar, where possible."

Ritz grunted.

I walked swiftly up the flagstone walkway to the front door.

Kitty and Angela Morton were seated in the living room at the back of the house. It was the first time I had met her. She was a petite blond, not unlike the current wife but at least a decade older. Guess the husband had a type.

We made quick introductions, using just our first names. I let Ritz hand Angela the necklace. No sense getting my prints on it too.

I nodded to Kitty, who gave me a thumbs-up. She seemed particularly pleased with this successful outcome. Her mouth was set in a determined smile.

Angela stared down at the necklace in her hand. "I can't thank you enough," she said, eyes shining. Diamonds dripped through her fingers. They graduated from small at the clasp to seriously impressive in the middle.

This was my favorite part. When we meet with our client to tell them the job is done… well, it makes my heart swell. We've done something good for someone.

Angela didn't let us down. She was effusive with praise. It was a pleasure to watch her pretty blond head bob in excitement.

"You guys…you're amazing! I never thought I would see it again. Thank you!"

Her smile lit up the room.

"You're very welcome," said Kitty. She was beaming.

I rose and reached for my purse. "Sorry to cut this short, but I'm here on my lunch break. I've got to get back to work."

"Where do you work?" asked Angela. Her eyes lifted from the necklace. They glittered like the diamonds.

"At the city animal shelter," I said.

"She's the donations manager and event coordinator," said Kitty proudly. Kitty is always generous when it comes to boosting my ego.

"I'll be sure to give a large donation this year," said Angela. She sounded sincere. "Thank you again!" She waved with her free hand.

Kitty walked Ritz and me to the door. "That's a job well done," she said with satisfaction.

I nodded with a smile. The good feeling stayed with me all the way back to work.

Sometimes it seems like the world doesn't care. But we do.

•••

The weekend passed quickly. It was another noisy Monday at the animal shelter when Alison appeared at my office door. She was practically bouncing.

"The puppies have come!" she said.

I popped up from my chair and followed her out to the kennels. This was the best part about working at the animal shelter. Puppies and kittens.

We had been alerted earlier that some kind children had discovered a shivering mom with her pups in an old shed. The kids' parents had informed the authorities, thankfully.

I could hear the puppies yipping as

I entered the shelter area. We hurried to the largest kennel room, at the back, and peeked over the half door. Four adorable shepherd/husky crosses, about seven weeks old, engaged in climbing over each other. I pulled open the half door and sat down. They made a mad dash for my lap. That always makes my heart sing. We played for a while, until one of them pooped. Then that took all their attention. I escaped while they were playing Let's All Try to Do That. Happily, Wanda, one of our animal-care workers, came to the rescue.

When I got back to my office, my cell phone dingled. The ring tone signaled Kitty's home phone. I answered immediately.

"Del, can you get here? Now? We have a problem." Her voice sounded unusually clipped.

"On my way." I hung up.

That was weird. Usually Kitty texted me.

What was so urgent that she felt she had to call instead?

I was at her front door in under ten minutes. I didn't even get a chance to ring the bell. The carved wooden door swept open, and Kitty stood there, looking miserable.

"What is it?" I asked, immediately alert. Had someone died?

"Follow me." She turned, leading the way into the living room.

I had to walk briskly to keep up, so I hardly noticed the priceless artwork that covered the walls. Kitty's place wasn't big, but it sure held the goods.

A woman was standing before the window, looking out on the forest view. She turned as she heard us approach.

I put her age at about fifty, but she had made a tremendous effort to look ten years younger. She was extremely well dressed in a slim-fitting sheath that would probably fetch four figures on Bloor Street in Toronto. Her shoulder-length caramel hair had been colored and styled by the very best.

It was her face that gave away her age. This was not a happy woman.

Kitty turned to me. Her eyes still had that wild look.

"Del, this is *Angela Morton*." She put special emphasis on the name.

I stared at Kitty. Then my gaze swung back to the woman before us.

I had never seen her before.

NINE

The real Mrs. Morton was very gracious. Frankly, I was surprised Jeff Morton had left her for such a lightweight like Cindy.

She was here, apparently, to discuss a hospital charity event with Kitty and was just leaving.

I waited until we were alone before losing my cool.

"*That* was Angela Morton," I repeated. "The real Angela Morton."

"Yes," said Kitty. She tugged nervously on the hem of her Chanel jacket.

"Then the woman who hired us to steal the necklace? And then came here to get it—"

"I don't know," said Kitty, throwing up her hands. "An imposter."

Holy crap. "A damned clever imposter," I said, flopping down on the leather couch.

I started to laugh then. Not a nice laugh. The sort that escapes you when you realize you are totally screwed and there is nothing you can do about it.

"Oh lordy. What a con. She just got us to steal a three-hundred-thousand-dollar necklace for her."

Kitty sat down, more gracefully than I had, in the cream chair opposite.

"It would seem so." Her voice held a coarse note I didn't hear often.

"And the hell of it is, we can't even report her to anyone." Certainly not the police.

Tell the police we had stolen a necklace for the wrong person?

Dang. It was the perfect scam. I groaned out loud.

"Does Ritz know yet?" I asked.

Kitty shook her head. "No one knows."

"Let's keep it that way for now." I wasn't looking forward to telling Ritz.

This totally sucked. I prided myself on being particularly wily. It was too bloody galling to be outsmarted by a stranger.

Kitty cleared her throat. "We need more checks and balances, obviously."

Closing the barn door after the horse had bolted. Poor Kitty. She was having a hard time keeping her emotions in check. Me, I never bothered trying. I said a few more choice words. "What are we going to do now?"

Kitty shrugged and looked miserable.

That put me in battle mode.

"Okay, where does this leave us? Let me

think." I shot up from the couch and started pacing. "One. The necklace has been reported stolen, right?"

"Probably. We don't know that for sure."

"*But*. The person who hired us to steal it is not likely to tell anyone we did it."

Kitty perked up. "No, she won't. As we speak, the necklace is probably being pulled apart so that it can be fenced.

"So. As long as we stay out of the frame, we're okay."

"What do you mean by that?"

"As long as the police don't find a trail leading to us, we should be safe."

Kitty frowned. "Maybe."

And as long as Mac didn't spill. I didn't think he would. Maybe I should keep in touch with him, just to make sure. I'd worry about that later.

I had enough on my mind right now. A despicable broad had bested me. Bad enough to get beat. I'm just fine with a fair fight though. But this smooth-faced imposter had deliberately pulled a fast one and was leaving us to take the blame if things went wrong.

I did not like that, not one bit.

I plunked back down on the couch. Then I got to thinking about who the imposter could be. I voiced this to Kitty.

"Someone who knew about the necklace, obviously," said Kitty. "And knew that it had belonged to Angela Morton's grandmother."

"Who would know that? Angela, of course. Maybe some of her relatives and close friends."

"The ex-husband," said Kitty.

"Cindy. The second wife would know. Probably her close friends too. Probably she gloated about it to them," I said.

Here's what I've learned about the sort of women who steal husbands. They view it as a challenge. See if they can win the man away from the home gal who has the advantage. So that necklace would be something like a trophy to Cindy Morton. She not only got the man, but she also robbed the first wife of something else that belonged to her. Something that went back even further than the husband. What a coup.

Wait a minute. Something was sitting at the back of my mind, tingling, trying to find its way out. *Work with it, Del,* I told myself. *Let it come free.*

I left the couch and started pacing again. "Kitty, we're missing something."

"Huh?" She looked up.

"A necklace worth several hundred thousand dollars? From your grandmother? Would you forget to include that in the divorce settlement?"

She shook her head. "I wouldn't forget any of my good jewelry. Not ever. Not even for a weekend."

No kidding. I only had two surplus diamond engagement rings, and no way would I forget—

Wait a minute.

And just like that, I had it. "Who told us about the necklace?" I spun to look at her. "The imposter wife, right?"

She was staring at me now. "Er...right."

"So who told us that tale about it being inherited from the grandmother?" I paused. "Also the imposter wife." I let it sink in.

Kitty straightened her back. "You mean..."

"Think about it." I picked up the pacing. It helped me think. "We bought this story about a poor ex-wife being robbed of her grandmother's jewelry. What if it *wasn't* the grandmother's? What if it wasn't the ex-wife's *at all*?"

Kitty rose to her feet. "You mean that..."

I nodded. "Would we have taken the case if it wasn't a sentimental story about dear granny leaving a necklace that got pilfered by the new wife? Of course we wouldn't."

"So," said Kitty, trying to work through it, "if it wasn't the real Angela Morton's grandmother's necklace, whose was it?"

"Cindy's, of course. The second wife's. We stole a necklace from the rightful owner and gave it to a complete stranger. And now we are all going to hell." If not prison first. I dropped to the couch with a groan.

I sat comatose for about thirty seconds. Then anger kicked in. "I'm going to get it back," I said.

"How?" asked Kitty, waving a hand in the air. "We don't even know who she is!"

"I'll find out," I said between gritted teeth. "Just watch me."

TEN

I was still fuming when I got back to the animal shelter. The cheery sound of yipping puppies greeted me as I pulled open the door. I peeked in on them and waved to Wanda before heading to my office. I was almost a pleasant human being again by the time I sat down in the worn desk chair.

"Hi," I said to Pepé, who had commandeered my guest chair. "You wouldn't believe what happened today."

Pepé Le Pew is an enormous fluffy black cat. He is called Pepé Le Pew for good reason—he has a bushy white tail and also has a tendency to toot very bad smells. This is the reason he is still at the shelter. He's been adopted twice and returned both times. Luckily, this is fine with him. He treats my office as his home and this whole building as his kingdom.

As office buddies go, he is neat and undemanding.

I called Ritz and told her to get over here when she could. I had news that wasn't suitable for the phone. Then I busied myself with paperwork. Pepé was totally occupied with napping. As I said, the perfect office buddy.

Ritz knocked on my office door about an hour later. She was about to sit down in the guest chair when I stopped her.

"Wait. Don't sit there." I pointed to the sleeping cat. "And don't try to move him."

"Why not?" asked Ritz. "Does he scratch?"

"Worse," I said. "A lot worse. There's a reason he's called Pepé Le Pew."

I saw the light dawn in her eyes. "After the cartoon skunk?"

I nodded. "*Skunk* being the operative word. Particularly bad if you try to lift him."

She leaned back against the wall. "I'm good here then."

I lost no time telling her about the imposter situation.

"Bummer," she said. "So the first wife was a fake. You need to locate her. Put a gun down her throat and make her cough up the necklace." She dropped her backpack of tools on the floor.

"Not quite so bloodthirsty, but that's the general picture." On second thought, nix the *not quite so*. I *was* feeling pretty bloodthirsty.

"Do we know her name?"

I shook my head sadly. "I was thinking we could check the pawn shops. And the fences known to the family. See if anyone contacts them. But it's a long shot, I admit. Chances are, she'll go far away to sell the necklace." If she sells it at all. Maybe she just wanted to sit on it as a trophy. I groaned.

Ritz shrugged. "It's an idea. But I have a much better one."

I waited.

"You still got that connection who works for the license bureau?"

"Not sure. Why?"

Ritz grinned. "'Cause I might have a license plate she can look up." She unhooked the smartphone from her belt and started thumbing it.

I sat up straight. "You took a photo of her car? When we were at Kitty's?"

"Damn straight. Here's the plate." She handed me the phone.

Sometimes Ritz surprised the heck out of me. "Oh darlin'. You are worth your weight in gold." I copied down the letters and numbers.

"How about diamonds," she said. I gave her back the phone. She hooked it to her belt. "Can't stay. I'm on a job." I watched her pick up her bag and go.

What job? I nearly yelled after her. Then I shook myself. *Don't even think about it.*

Things were looking up. I had the imposter's license-plate number. That meant I could probably trace her name and address. With any luck, she would be in the area.

Of course, I wasn't going to do the trace *myself.* That would take forever. Sometimes having a big happy family comes in handy. Okay, not necessarily happy. But big.

I got out my drugstore untraceable phone and called Gina. I used her burner phone number, not the smartphone. I knew she had both. When the burner phone buzzed, she would know it was family. She would know it was business, if you get my drift.

We didn't bother with pleasantries. "It's Del. Does your cousin Theresa still work at the license bureau?"

"Yup," said Gina. "I'll tell her to call you at this number." She rang off. That was the good thing about Gina. She didn't have to know everything.

Through her job, Theresa had access to a lot of interesting intel. This was particularly valuable if your extended family was into car theft.

My smartphone rang. It appeared I didn't need to think about how to keep tabs on Mac. He'd beat me to it.

"It's Mac," said the voice on the phone. My heartbeat seemed to stumble. "I've suddenly got a lot of new requests for building security work. My sales team is going mad with quotes. Just looking at the names on here, it's clear I have you to thank for it."

"Me?" I was baffled. I hadn't said anything to anyone. So it must have been Kitty who'd mobilized the family to give Mac more business. But I couldn't tell Mac about Kitty. As far as he knew, only Ritz and I were involved in the burglary.

"Well, hey!" I said with a little laugh. "Friends help out friends, you know."

"Glad to hear we're friends," Mac said easily. His voice seemed to do something to my insides. "I think *friends* should meet for dinner. You free tonight?"

I gulped. "Let me check. Oops, I have an incoming call on my other phone. Call you back."

Okay, that was cowardly. I was a complete coward around men these days. But I really did have an incoming call. It was Theresa. I told her the license-plate number, and she told me to wait. Within minutes she was back with the goods. I rang off with satisfaction and called Kitty with the news. She said to be at her place at six, and to come alone.

Mac phoned back twice before six. I didn't answer. *Coward, coward, coward...*

ELEVEN

At six, I pulled up in front of Kitty's place. She had told me to come alone. So I was sort of surprised to see an unfamiliar black Charger in the driveway. The kind that could outrun a red Mustang. I had to force myself to walk past it to the front door. Fast cars are my weakness, and I'm not good with temptation.

The door was unlocked, so I walked right in.

"Hello?"

"We're back here," yelled Kitty.

I plunked my purse down on the bench and continued down the hall. I stopped dead in the doorway.

The living room had become one big spiderweb. And that was me, the fly, looking directly at the spider.

"Hi, Red." Mac grinned at me. He was standing by the back window, holding a beer. "You look good in civvies." He eyed my slim jeans and wraparound red blouse.

"For crissake!" I turned to Kitty. "A little warning maybe?"

She shrugged her small shoulders and looked innocent. But I knew better. I was beginning to suspect Kitty had an agenda beyond the job at hand.

"I needed the advice of a security expert," she said. "Since there was already one involved with this case..."

I plunked down on the cream couch. "But can he be trusted?"

She waved away my concern with her hand and became all businesslike. "That's taken care of. We have mutual business interests. Now listen to this, Del. We've been doing research. We know our con artist's name is Maria Perez. No police record. Hardly any personal info. It's probably one of her aliases."

"She rents a small bungalow in Aldershot," said Mac. "Right in the middle of don't-notice-me land." Aldershot was a leafy suburb on the lake, peopled mainly by retired folk.

"Unlikely to be much security, according to Mac here. It's a rental, after all," said Kitty. "Landlords don't pay for extras."

I nodded. She would know, being a landlord herself.

Mac leaned back against the sliding glass doors. "You'd be surprised how many thieves don't bother to secure their own homes. Must think they're the only bad guys around, for some reason."

I watched him with interest. Perhaps he had something there. First thing next week, I was going to look into increasing security for my little condo.

I addressed Kitty again. "So. What's your plan? How do we get her out of the house?"

Kitty smiled. "Leave that to me. She will be out of the house tomorrow night."

I cocked my head at her. I could ask what she had in mind. Or I could let it go. Did I really need to know everything?

Kitty had lots of connections I didn't know about. Probably I didn't want to know about them.

Safer to let it go.

"Okay," I said. "So we make plans for tomorrow night. I can understand why you would want to pick Mac's brain about the likelihood of us running into trouble with security systems. But why is he still here?"

Kitty reached for her wineglass on the glass coffee table. "Well, that's exactly it, Del. These are just educated guesses. We can't predict everything."

I grinned. "So you've conned him into coming along with me to steal back the necklace. For security reasons. To sweep and protect." I chuckled at my own joke.

"What?" asked Mac.

I turned to him. "Haven't you figured it out yet? She's got you playing Little John to my Robin Hood. Welcome to the Merry Band."

"Del," said Kitty. "Stop torturing the poor man."

Mac looked like he had been hit by a truck. "I need to talk to her alone. Do you mind?" he said to Kitty.

A satisfied smile spread across her face. "Be my guest. I'll be in the kitchen."

We watched her amble into the hall and shut the door behind her.

Mac turned back to me.

"Are you completely nuts?" he said.

It was nice to see our relationship had progressed to this stage.

"You don't have to come along," I said reasonably. "That was Kitty's idea, not mine. I can do this alone with Ritz." We'd certainly done things like it before. Not always successfully, mind you.

I decided to get a little devious. "Dino won't be there, if that's what's worrying you. He's stuck in New York." I counted on the fact that Mac hadn't forgotten who'd given him the broken nose.

He glared at me. His voice got lower and meaner. "I'm not worried about Dino. I'm a big boy. I can take care of myself."

Bull's-eye! I had to hide my smile. No man likes to be reminded of a fight he didn't win. Looking at him now, I had no doubt Mac could hold his own against any of my relatives. He obviously worked out. I felt a rush of desire. *Control yourself, Del.*

He was taut like a spring now. Kept hitting one big fist against the palm of his other hand.

"It's one thing to keep my mouth shut about things that don't concern me." He was talking about not reporting us to the police after that earlier job, no doubt.

He continued. "And it's one thing to provide advice from a distance. Happy to do that for a good client like your aunt. I'm a security pro. Hell, I *manage* a security company."

"A really good one," I agreed. "All my uncles agree."

Mac shot me another look. It was wicked of me to play the uncle card, I admit.

"I get a lot of business from your family. But this goes a little beyond the usual service agreement."

I cleared my throat. "It's merely a different type of surveillance. You could tell us what we need to avoid. From a safe distance. Outside. You wouldn't have to go into the house. Just look the place over. Let me know the score." I was beginning to see the wisdom in it. Kitty was right. We could use an expert set of eyes. Also a lookout, since Dino wasn't going to be there.

Mac frowned. "And I would be doing this...why? Other than to keep in good with your family."

"To bring a bit of justice to the world. To take down a really evil con artist." I pointed a finger at him. "Maria Perez is bad through and through. I hate people who steal from others." I hated even more the people who tried to pull one over on me. But that was a given.

bibliotheca SelfCheck System
Orinda Library
Contra Costa County Library
26 Orinda Way
Orinda, Ca. 94563
925-254-2184

Customer ID: **************

Items that you checked out

Title: :The B-team : the case of the angry first wif
ID: 31901062575297
Due: Saturday, October 15, 2022
Messages:
Item checked out.

Title: Lila /
ID: 31901054456266
Due: Saturday, October 15, 2022
Messages:
Item checked out.

Total items: 2
Account balance: $0.00
9/24/2022 2:55 PM
Ready for pickup: 0

Renew online or by phone
ccclib.org
1-800-984-4636

Have a nice day!

I had to appeal to his code of honor. My pride was at stake, so I ramped up the pleading. "Come on, Mac! Where's your sense of justice? We're doing a good thing with this job. We're going to take back that necklace and return it to its rightful owner."

Those warm brown eyes squinted at me. "How do I know you're *really* going to give back the necklace instead of just keeping it yourself?"

"Don't be stupid." Now I did sound exasperated.

He folded his arms across his chest. "Explain."

I said each word slowly, as if talking to a child. "If we were going to keep the necklace, we would have done so in the first place. Instead of handing it over to Maria."

It took a few seconds for that to sink in. Then he nodded. "Fair enough."

"So you're in?" I watched his face carefully.

There was a moment of awkward silence. He ran a big hand through his thick hair.

"I'm not exactly sure why I'm doing this," he said.

"There's another reason. Because you have the hots for me and have since high school," I said brightly.

He barked a harsh laugh. "Tell me the plan," he said.

TWELVE

I told him the plan.

"I always had a thing for Robin Hood. And particularly for Maid Marian," he said at last.

"Which reminds me. We should all wear black hoodies. And dark glasses."

"I thought you said there was no chance of being caught," said Mac.

Oops. "Hardly any chance. This way, hardly any chance of being identified either."

"From a distance," said Mac. He folded his arms across his chest.

"Do you really plan to stick around for a close-up?" I shot back. "Mac, if you're afraid, you don't have to do this."

"I'm not afraid. I'm just..." He struggled for words. "You're a complete wacko. You know that, right?"

"Not at all," I said primly. "I'm merely an ordinary gal who sees a lot of wrong happening in the world and wants to right it."

"*Ordinary.*" Mac shook his head. "Are all the women in your family so damned fearless?"

"Wait until you meet my mother." I shivered for effect.

It took about an hour to go over all the details with Kitty. After that, Mac and I left the house together. I could almost feel the heat from his body as he walked beside me.

I snuck a glance at him, catching the strong body and rugged face in profile.

The night air was crisp, but I felt uncomfortably warm all over.

I lingered by his Charger as he clicked open the lock.

"Hot car," I said. "Hope you have good security on that."

Mac gave me that crooked smile. "Why? Are you planning to steal it?"

I turned back to my car. "Nope. I like my Pony. Suits me."

"A red Mustang. How fitting." Mac shook his head. "I always had a thing for wild horses."

"Can't be tamed," I said, walking over to the driver's side.

"Now *that* sounds like a challenge," Mac said softly.

• • •

It was dark. It was the next night. I was feeling antsy.

"I wish Dino was back," I said.

Ritz looked over at me. "Why? He's not a security whiz like this Mac guy."

"I don't know," I said, hugging my arms to my chest. "I'm getting bad vibes."

"Oh no." Ritz groaned. "Not another one of your premonitions."

"That's why I wish Dino was here. He takes my premonitions seriously." *Unlike some people*, I said to myself.

We had parked down the road from Maria Perez's house. It was a really quiet street. Not a soul in sight. As per the plan, Mac was going to drive a Stonehouse Security van and park it in the driveway. That way, we would look semi-legit if anyone saw us lurking around the place.

In the rearview mirror of the Mustang, I saw Mac pull the van into the driveway. "Let's go," I said to Ritz. I flung myself out of the car and pocketed the keys. I left the doors unlocked in case we needed to get away quickly.

Mac had gone the whole route. Not only did he have the van, but he was wearing a Stonehouse Security jacket and a ballcap with the company logo on it. I stayed back across the street as he walked up the sidewalk to the front door.

I couldn't see what he was doing there, but he didn't stay very long. I saw him go around the corner of the house to check the side door and a few windows. A few minutes later he joined us across the street.

"The place is clean. No security system. Just a deadbolt on the front door."

"I can take care of that," said Ritz.

Mac looked at me, all curious.

I shrugged. "Her dad owns The Lock on Locke. You know, the locksmiths in Hamilton."

"I can open anything," said Ritz. "And this doesn't even take explosives."

I saw Mac swallow.

"Are you carrying...?" he said.

"No, she isn't," I said. I hoped she wasn't. "Come on, Ritz. Mac, you stay in the van, like you're writing up an order. Text me if you see trouble coming."

"Will do," he said.

Ritz and I waited for him to cross the street and disappear into the van. Then we scooted across the street and up the sidewalk.

The house was all in darkness. It was one of those low yellow-brick bungalows that would have been desirable in the 1960s. Not huge but neat and well kept on the outside. Completely unremarkable. Thus perfect for staying under the radar.

I took all this in as Ritz tripped the

lock with her tools. It took less than three minutes. I timed her, as is my habit. Ridiculous how easy that was for her to do.

We hurried into the house and closed the door behind us. We didn't need to turn on the lights because the streetlight shone through the front window.

"Check the bedrooms," I said. "I'll do the fridge."

Ritz nodded and scurried down the hall.

I could see the kitchen off to the left. It's a curious thing, but many people hide their valuables in plastic containers in the freezer. They think it's safer than a bedroom. This house might have a freezer downstairs, but I was counting on the fact that it was a rental. No extras included.

It was an old-fashioned fridge in an equally dated kitchen. The freezer was on the top, unlike in most appliances sold today. I opened it. Hardly anything there. A few microwave dinners and ice-cube trays. Sort of like mine at home.

I closed the freezer and pulled out a kitchen chair to wait for Ritz.

I could have continued searching, but honestly, Ritz was better at it than I was. And chances were, she'd find something in the master bedroom.

So I looked around the kitchen and wondered what it would be like to live there. With a husband and family. Children. Did I want children? Yes, I had to admit I'd always wanted kids. And I was getting on. Thirty-five was staring me in the face. Time was running out.

But you needed a husband to have kids. Well, at least a man, for part of the process.

Then I wondered about Mac. Did he want kids?

Bad train of thought, I scolded myself. But I couldn't resist. Maybe he did have kids. I'd never asked him. Had he been married before? I needed to ask Kitty. She'd know, or she could find out. I could text her. She was on standby anyway, ready to text me if anything went wrong at her end.

That's when I realized I had left my cell phone in the car.

Crap. It would be sitting there in the cup holder, having a nice little sleep. It wouldn't alert me to anything.

I groaned. Served me right for being so infatuated with a man. I only ever slipped up when my mind was on a man.

Everything is okay, I told myself. *You can check by peeking out the front door.* I rose from the chair and started for the foyer.

"Here, catch!" said Ritz. She was already in the hall. I put my hands up in time to catch a small flannel sack with a drawstring.

"Damn you, Ritz! I might have dropped it."

"Diamonds don't break," she said.

I loosened the drawstring and peered in

the bag. "Holy shit, Ritz. There's more than our necklace in here."

"Insurance," she said.

I was going to quiz her about what she meant by that when I heard a sound.

The door swung open before I could reach it. Mac stood on the front step, and he wasn't alone. Maria Perez was directly behind him, and she had a gun.

THIRTEEN

"Get inside." Maria poked the gun into Mac's back.

Mac walked over the door sill and into the hall. His face was a portrait in fury. I had obviously missed a few texts. But he had allowed himself to be caught while on sentry duty. That was a whole lot worse. I would have felt sorry for him, but I was doing my best to clear my head of all emotion.

I needed a clear head.

Maria kept the gun steady as she closed the door behind her. I couldn't tell the make of gun from here, but it looked like she knew how to use it.

"I thought you were mob," said Maria, looking at me. "Your big boy here seems like a novice. What are you doing, running a daycare?"

I could see Mac stiffen at that.

I shrugged. "Everyone has to start somewhere."

So far, Maria had seen only me. I was holding the bag of goodies. Ritz had retreated back into the shadows behind her.

Hopefully, Maria wouldn't even know Ritz was there.

"Put the jewelry down," Maria said. Her voice was ice cold.

I should have been scared. In truth, my heart was beating triple time. But I'd go to hell and back before I'd show fear to this dame.

"Nope," I said. All eyes swung to me.

Ritz moved a little to the right. She could take Maria out with a karate chop, I knew. But she had to get close enough to reach her.

"The jewelry." Maria gestured with her free hand. "Put it on the table there, or I'll shoot."

I glanced at the little hall table. Then I looked back at her. "Nope," I said again.

"Huh?" Maria said.

"No you won't." I shrugged again. Big, nonchalant shrug. Like I didn't have a care in the world.

"Won't what?" asked Mac. He was clearly baffled. Probably from having watched too many cop shows. They always get it wrong in cop shows.

"Won't shoot," I said with confidence. I turned back to address Maria. "See? There are two of us. You can maybe shoot one of us. But the other will jump you. And we're mob-trained," I said. Well, I was. I didn't know about Mac. "So you won't leave this room alive." I was actually relishing this moment.

"And you're willing to take that chance?" The gun moved to aim at me.

"Sweetheart, more to the point, are you?" I was pretty sure about this. "You kill me, he kills you. No question about that. So we're no further ahead. Is this a good day to die, sister?"

The gun drooped a bit. She was clearly thinking it through. We all waited in silence.

"So what do you suggest?" she said.

Think, Del. Think! "A compromise. We take the Morton necklace. You get to keep the rest of the haul. We all go home happy." Except she was already home. And she didn't look very happy.

I was right about that. This woman didn't look sane. A black look crossed her face. "No, I don't think so," she said. Her eyes shone like a madwoman's, and she lifted the gun.

Zzzzzttt!

"Eep." Maria fell to the floor. The gun dropped beside her.

Ritz stood directly behind her. Her hand was raised.

"A *Taser*? Ritz, where the hell did you get a Taser?" I asked.

She shrugged. "Guy I know." This shouldn't have surprised me. Ritz knew a lot of people whom you wouldn't want to know your address.

"Good work," I said, reaching down for Maria's gun. "Moving around her like that to get in position."

"Piece of cake," she said. "You don't have to get right up to a vic to use a Taser. Just get within range."

Mac came to life. He jerked forward as if to touch Maria. Then he wisely stopped himself and stared down at the body. "Is she dead?"

I asked the person most likely to know. "Ritz?"

"Don't think so," said Ritz, pocketing her weapon. "Not planning to stick around to find out. You got the goods?"

I held up the sack. Mac stared at me. He was surprisingly calm about all this, considering. "Are we just taking the Morton necklace?"

It was my turn to grin. I really wanted to get back at this dame. "We take the bundle. Because I've got a cunning plan."

FOURTEEN

Mac offered to drive me home. I think he wanted to talk alone. So I let Ritz take my car. When he stopped in front of my place, I didn't invite him in. We didn't kiss, and he didn't propose marriage to me. But we did make a plan to meet for dinner in two days' time.

"You owe me," said Mac. "Somewhere expensive, like La Paloma."

Not exactly the most romantic thing in the world to say. But I was a realist. This could be the beginning of an okay relationship. He might even be a keeper. Heck, he could turn out to be loser number three.

It was just after ten, so I wasted no time. I phoned my cousin Gina on the burner phone.

"If I wanted to get a parcel to the editor of the *Steeltown Star* without leaving a trace, how would I go about doing it?"

"Just a sec," said Gina. "I'll ask Pete."

Pete is now the sports reporter for the local paper. He's a great guy. He even puts up with the family. Not that I'm surprised. I'm sure he'd agree that Gina is worth it.

She came back on the line. "Here's what to do." And then she told me.

"Thanks," I said. "Don't you even want to know what's in the parcel?"

"Nope," she said. "Safer if I don't."

I laughed. Gina was a pro at the family business.

"Besides," she continued, "if you're involved, it's probably going to be on the front page of the paper."

Funny she would say that. I was still smiling when I hung up.

I put on plastic gloves for this job. I helped the little sack release its contents on my kitchen counter. Four diamond necklaces, each a stunner. Every one worth more than most people lived on in a year. Gorgeous things. Gina would have been salivating.

I put them all in a puffy padded envelope. I addressed the parcel as Gina instructed. But I was never one to do things the simple way. As my mother would say, I always like to "put a fringe around the edge."

So I included a small note.

Please return these to their rightful owners, with my compliments. Robin Hoodie

Then I went to bed.

• • •

The phone rang at six on Thursday morning. I am not usually awake by six. I am certainly not civil.

"Are you completely nuts?"

It sounded like Mac's voice, with a side order of laughter.

"Huh," I said into the phone (which loosely translates to "most likely").

"Have you seen today's headline?" Yup, definitely Mac. "*Robin Hoodie is a Hero!*"

I could almost hear him smiling and shaking his head.

I sat up. "Read the rest," I said, more lucidly.

He quoted: "*A fortune in stolen jewelry mailed to the editorial offices of the Steeltown Star has everyone asking the question, Who is Robin Hoodie?*"

I smiled. He read more. I was in bliss mode, just listening to his voice. This job had turned out right. We had bested a con artist. A really diabolical one. Those jewels would be going back to their rightful owners. It was a glorious feeling.

But I knew it wouldn't last. The feeling of triumph would wear off soon. I was always a little sorry when a job was completed.

Mac rang off, still chuckling. Luckily, I had dinner with him to look forward to. I'd report back to the rest of the B-Team before then. Chances were, they would already have seen the paper.

I had drunk my starter coffee when Kitty phoned at seven.

"Nice work," she said.

I was inordinately pleased. "I thought you would like the Robin Hoodie touch." Robin was my middle name. Not even Ritz knew that.

"You wore gloves, of course."

"For both the job and the packaging." The annoyance came through in my voice.

"I'm not a complete newbie."

"I trained you well," she said. Figured she would find a way to take credit. "I have another job for the B-Team. Someone has been preying on seniors again. Meet me here at nine tonight. Oh, and bring Mac. My intel says you're seeing him tonight." A pause. "I like that lad." She hung up.

I smiled into the phone.

ACKNOWLEDGMENTS

I suppose I should thank actor George Peppard. The leader of *The A-Team* was my kind of guy. I grew up with that show and, from the beginning, was determined to form my own vigilante group. I became a writer instead but never forgot that original goal. And so *The B-Team* now has life in print.

Many thanks to my wonderful set of writer friends who are my beta readers: Cathy Astolfo, Janet Bolin, Alison Bruce,

Cheryl Freedman, Joan O'Callaghan and Nancy O'Neill. You all know how much I cherish your support and encouragement.

More thanks to Ruth Linka and her team at Orca Books. They take my manuscripts and make them sing. They are my A-team.

Melodie Campbell got her start writing stand-up comedy. Her fiction has been described by editors and reviewers as "wacky" and "laugh-out-loud funny." Winner of ten awards, including the 2014 Derringer and the 2014 Arthur Ellis for *The Goddaughter's Revenge*, Melodie has over two hundred publishing credits, including forty short stories and thirteen novels. She is the former executive director of Crime Writers of Canada. She lives outside Toronto, Ontario. For more information, visit www.melodiecampbell.com.

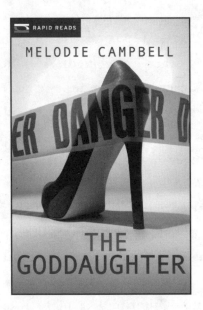

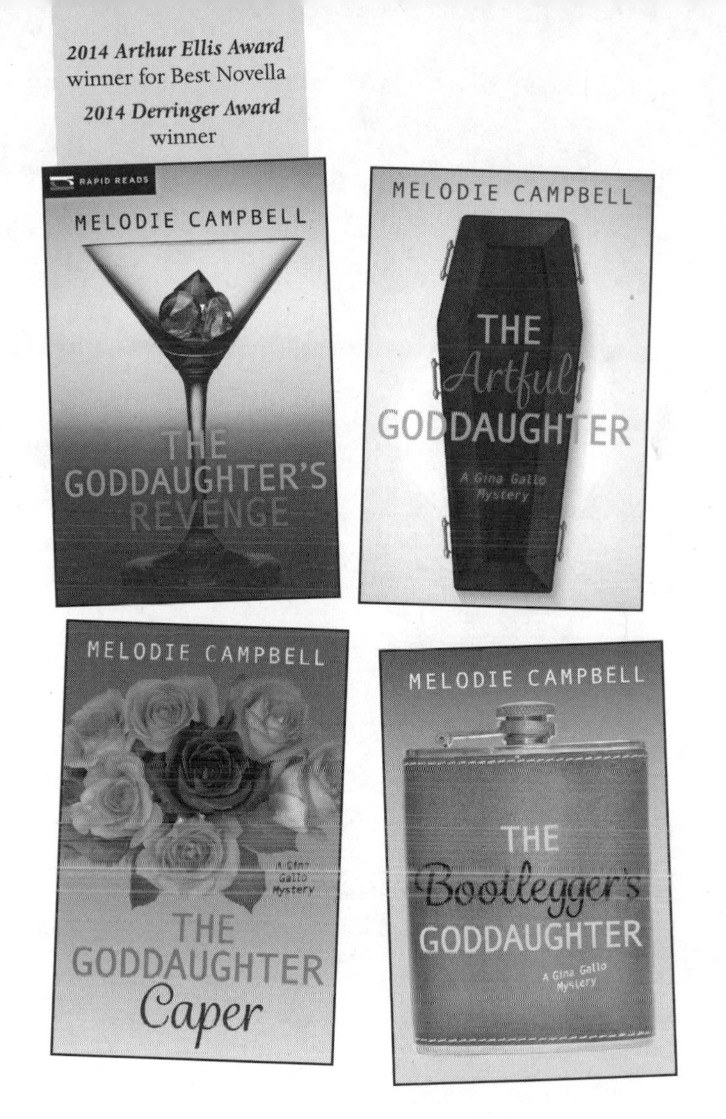

"The finest compact mystery series out there."
—*Canadian Mystery Reviews*

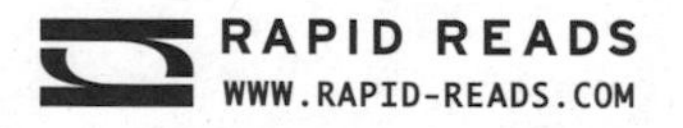